Oh! How Things Change!

Oh! How Things Change!

Aleasher Hightower

Acknowledgments

First and foremost, I acknowledge my parents Douglas and Obbie Hightower for always being supportive.

I'm appreciative to my dad for working hard and taking the time out to talk to me about life. As a little girl, I frequently interrupted him while he was cutting the grass to come sit down to have a tea party with me, and he never complained. And I am blessed to have had such a great example of a man for my father.

I also thank my mom for staying in my ear, about not only being book smart, but having common sense that is needed to get me through life's roller coaster ride. I thank her for being a positive role model. As a child, she made sure I had a warm breakfast every day, and had dinner ready every day when I made it home from school.

I also must acknowledge my three older brothers that felt the need to speak to me about dudes, dating and not being green or stupid when it came to guys. I can say that the knowledge they enlightened me on kept me woke, and I will be forever grateful. And to my parents and my siblings, may you all rest in peace and I'll see you all on the other side!

I also thank and deeply appreciate my son, grandsons, family members, and friends for your love and support, and last but not least, I must sincerely thank my cast members and staging team who are my extended family, I love how they brought the characters and set to life when I produced, "Oh! How Things Change!" into a stage play.

Thank you all, and I dedicate this book to every one of you!

Love,
Aleasher

Book Cover Design by Macdezignz

Intro

This narrative gives a glimpse into the fast life, aka street life, aka the game, but it reveals that all that glitters isn't gold. This book was transformed and inspired by a play that the author wrote and later turned into a screenplay and now a book. Although this book is fiction, it gives insight into the lifestyles of some of Richmond California's pimps, playas, hustlers and prostitutes. Most Richmond Pimps started having their females work the streets of Oakland, San Francisco and towns en route to Los Angeles, California and Las Vegas. Let the narrative be awareness so that you can educate the young adults, and even sometimes teenagers, to detour them from this path.

Intro

This narrative gives a glimpse into the fast life, aka street life, aka the game, but it reveals that all that glitters isn't gold. This book was transformed and inspired by a play that the author wrote and later turned into a screenplay and now a book. Although this book is fiction, it gives insight into the lifestyles of some of Richmond California's pimps, playas, hustlers and prostitutes. Most Richmond Pimps started having their females work the streets of Oakland, San Francisco and towns en route to Los Angeles, California and Las Vegas. Let the narrative be awareness so that you can educate the young adults, and even sometimes teenagers, to detour them from this path.

It's Friday evening, at 6:00 pm., the summer of 1984. Twenty-four-year-old Tre is sitting in a bar called *The Spot* in Oakland, California, on the Track. The Track is where the prostitutes work. He has a clear view of the Track from the huge window that covers the entire wall. Richmond, California pimps, as well as pimps from the Bay Area, international pimps, and hustlers hang out on the San Pablo Track. Twenty-two-year-old Money D walks in and heads toward Tre. Tre gets up, they embrace and Money D says, "What's up?" Tre replies, "Money D, man, just watching my workers." Money D responds, "That's what we do!" They laugh, and Money D sits down across from Tre. Tre's hair is permed with curls, he's wearing a tailored burgundy suit, white shirt, and burgundy alligator shoes that match his suit. He's wearing all gold jewelry, a solid gold chain, a bracelet, and a gold and diamond pinky ring. Money D is wearing a pair of blue jeans with a bright green, long sleeve silk shirt and a pair of green alligator shoes, with gold jewelry as well, but his pinky ring is a solid gold nugget.

Twenty-one-year-old Dominic and his twenty-one-year-old broad named Beautiful pull up on the Track in a 1980 Brougham Cadillac, and park right across the street from the bar, *The Spot*, where Tre and Money D are at. Dominic is wearing a tailor-made blue *jean* suit, the jacket is long and stops right at his knee, with a multi-colored shirt, with blue alligator shoes to match his jean suit. Beautiful has long hair with curls, she's wearing a yellow tight-fitting dress, yellow shoes, matching yellow hoop earrings, and a yellow and gold necklace with a gold diamond ring.

Dominic goes in his jean jacket pocket, pulls out a folded-up dollar bill, opens it and takes his pinky finger, which has the gold ring, and scoops up some cocaine with his fingernail, and takes a snort up each nostril, then folds the remainder of the coke back up, and puts it back into his pocket. Dominic sees a street level dope dealer named Snake and grabs his gun from under the driver's seat, Beautiful says, "Dominic don't!" He looks very stern at her and says, "Stay out my business!" He jumps out the car and walks toward Snake. The usual pimps, playas and hustlers, which includes dope dealers, are on the Track. Tre and Money D can see Dominic approach Snake. Dominic rapidly steps to him, and is repeatedly yelling, "Snake!" Snake sees Dominic and starts walking away fast, acting like he doesn't hear him. Dominic stops walking and shouts, "I guess I'm going to have to shoot you in the back, since you can't hear!" Snake stops and quickly turns to face Dominic, and says, "Hey, Dominic, I just got back from out of town, I was gonna call you." Dominic starts walking toward Snake and replies, "Where's my money?" Snake responds, "I got robbed, man!" Dominic says, "You think I'm a sucka?" Snake touches his nose and says, "Nah, man, who said that?" Dominic replies, "I did!" Dominic shoots Snake in the leg, then goes in Snake's pockets, takes his money and his dope, and tells him, "You better get me the rest of my money, even these playas out here know who to play with." Snake is on the ground, scared, grabbing his leg and yelling, and screaming, "Okay, man!" Dominic slowly walks back to his Cadillac, counting the money, he gets into the car. Beautiful looks at him, and then shakes her head back and forth. Tre and Money D look at each other, and understand what just happened without saying a word, because the word has been out that Dominic been looking for Snake, so they're not shocked. Everyone knows the rules of the game. Nobody on the track will call the police, and Snake knows not to put the police in street business or the next time, he might not live to see another day. No one wants the Track hot, that slows down everybody's money.

Twenty-year-old Jazzy, who is a prostitute, walks into *The Spot*, sees Tre and stares at him, and goes to sit at the bar. Money D notices her watching Tre and says, "Every time we come to the set that chick stays eye bawling you." Tre looks at her and replies, "They call her Jazzy, she can look all she wants, until she has some choosing fees, that's all I'm gonna allow her to do, and she must don't have no real man, or her eyes would be in check." Money D responds, "I should have known you already peeped her or had some words with her." Money D gets up and says, "Hey Tre, I'm out of here, I got some business up." They embrace and Money D leaves. Jazzy walks up to Tre and pulls a thick envelope from her breast, and sits it on the table in front of him. Tre looks inside the envelope and says, "You sure you ready to choose me?" Jazzy answers, "Yeah, I've been watching you for a while, I like how you carry yourself, how you dress and the respect you get. And other pimps know not to step on you." Tre asks, "Who you with?" Jazzy says, "Nobody." Tre says, "So, I don't have to serve nobody no news that you with me now?" Jazzy replies, "That's right." Tre looks at Jazzy with a serious face and tells her, "There are rules to my pimping, anything any other pimp taught you before today, erase that from your mind, because that might land you in trouble with me. Just like pimps know

I don't play, any female that is with me needs to know that goes triple for them. Now, your choosing fee was right, but I need you to know, I need to see that kind of money coming in every night. Now, if that's going to be a problem, then let me know and you can walk, but the package is staying, because you out of pocket for stepping to a pimp like me anyway." Jazzy replies, "I heard about how serious you are, I know what it requires to be with you and I'm going to do whatever it takes to make that happen daily." Tre responds, "You still staying at that motel a few blocks from here?" Jazzy looks shocked that he knows where she is staying, Tre smiles as she answers, "Yes." Tre tells her to write down her number, she grabs a pin out of her purse and writes it on a napkin on the table. Tre says, "Tomorrow, you'll meet the rest of the family, but right now it's time to go to work."

The next day, Tre and Jazzy enter the house where his other two prostitutes live in the Hilltop area of Richmond. Jazzy has a purse on her shoulder, and is pulling a suitcase and holding a tote bag in her other hand. Twenty-four-year-old Candy and Twenty-two-year-old Precious are lying on the couch sleeping, but Candy is startled and wakes up as she hears Jazzy laughing, as she enters the house with Tre. Candy notices Tre and says, "Hey, daddy." Precious also wakes up and says, "Hi, baby." Tre introduces Jazzy, then tells her to have a seat. Tre begins to lay down the rules by saying, "This is our family. Trust no other female on the track. Every time you date a trick, give your money to Candy." Candy waves her hand so Jazzy will know who she is.

Tre looks at the other female and says, "That's Precious." Jazzy says, "Hi," Precious looks at her crazy and replies, "Hi," in a very low tone. Tre tells Jazzy, "If you have any problems, call me and go straight to Candy." Jazzy replies, "Okay." Tre's phone rings, he looks at his phone, answers and says, "Hey, Money D, hold on a minute." Tre says to the females, "I want y'all on the Track by 7:00, not 7:01." Tre turns to leave, gets back on the phone with a smile on his face, and says, "What's up?" Tre listens, stops smiling, and replies, "I'm on my way," and rushes out the door.

--$--

An hour later, Twenty-six-year-old Wayne, who used to be a pimp, is sitting on the couch rolling a joint of weed laced with cocaine, when Eighteen-year-old Nondo, a street level dope dealer, knocks on his door. Wayne is startled and stops rolling the joint. He gets up and shouts, "Who is it," as he approaches the door. Wayne looks through the peephole and sees who it is, the person replies, "Nondo." Wayne opens the door with a smile on his face, but when he opens the door Nondo is gone. Money D steps through the door wearing a black hoodie, blue jeans, and a ski mask, Money D immediately points his gun in Wayne's face. Then Tre walks in wearing all black, a ski mask, and his gun in his hand. Tre closes the front door and stands facing Wayne, and puts his finger up to his lips, which lets Wayne know, he better not say a word. Money D turns with his gun pointed and walks through the entire apartment, then returns to the living room and nods to Tre, indicating that there is no one else in the apartment. Tre takes off his mask, then Money D takes his off.

Wayne is scared! Tre steps closer to Wayne with a stern face and says, "You thought you could send my little soldiers to rob my auntie's house! You think I got some money in her house?" Wayne is shaking and replies, "Man…" Tre points the gun in Wayne's face and Wayne stops talking. Tre says, "Man, please don't tell me you are still mad that I knocked you for Candy." Tre shakes his head and tells Wayne, "Suckers really don't need to be in the game. Wayne, these youngsters love me and mine! You see, they got word to me, and me being here, and my auntie's house not touched, tells you how they feel about you!" Tre shoots Wayne in the face, then he and Money D pull their masks back down and leave out the back door.

--$--

That early evening, Candy is lounging on the couch, Jazzy is filing her fingernails, and Precious is observing Jazzy. Jazzy asks, "Where does Tre sleep?" Candy responds, "He has another spot." Jazzy replies, "I've always stayed with my man." Candy says, "He likes his space, we see him every day, so there ain't no problem." Precious tells them, "I like my space too, it's like when he's around, you have to always be in pocket." Candy looks at Precious and replies, "You would want to be in pocket even when he's not around." Precious says, "I'm not being disrespectful. Although I've been with him for three years, I still get nervous around him and I feel like I don't know him." Candy tells Precious, "You use to mess with those weak pimps that run their mouth like a walking douche bag. But those are the same ones that get disrespected by real pimps like Tre, ain't that why you left your last man?" Candy continues by saying, "I'm just glad he doesn't beat me for breakfast, lunch and dinner. My last man turned into a powder head. He snorted coke 24/7 and was paranoid I was gonna leave him, which I did!" Candy and the other females laugh. Candy then says, "I left after he became a powder head, and now I don't have to worry about pimps coming up to me every five minutes on the track saying…" Candy playfully gets in Precious face acting like a pimp and says, "You need to be friends with a real pimp!" They all laugh again. Precious replies, "Girl, that's real talk, I just can't find the right words to express how I'm really feeling." Jazzy asks Candy, "How long you been with Tre." Candy responds, "Almost five years," then waves her hand and says, "alright y'all, enough about all that, let's go the store and get some drank." Candy does a little dance and says, "So we can have some cocktails while getting dressed." Jazzy replies, "Let's roll." Precious says, "I'm going to stay here, I'll give y'all some money on the drank," then reaches in her pocket. Jazzy replies, "I got it, it's on me tonight." Precious responds, "Cool." Candy and Jazzy leaves and Precious looks out the window in deep thought.

--$--

Four months later, Beautiful is riding with her friend Jackie. Jackie is twenty-four years old and is not in the game. She manages her family's Beauty Supply Store in Richmond, California. Jackie is driving down Cutting Boulevard in Richmond, and Beautiful is on the passenger side. She gets on the freeway heading to Oakland, California and asks Beautiful, "Why are you so quiet." Beautiful replies, "It's been four months since Dominic went to jail for having a couple of bags of powder cocaine that the police found in his car, and when he gets out, he's eventually going back to jail, because he has a cocaine habit." Jackie looks shocked and says, "He uses his own product? Now I see why you were trying to leave him before he went to jail." Beautiful says, "Right! But once he went to jail, I knew it wasn't the right time to leave him, and believe me, he's not going to stop snorting. So earlier today, I told him, I'm done! Girl, I had to end our relationship." Jackie says, "I see why you are moving on, last week when you asked me about Tre, I knew something wasn't cool with you and Dominic." Beautiful nods her head in agreement. Jackie says, "You and Dominic did look good together, but I understand, friend." Jackie turns the music up to lift Beautiful's spirit and they both start singing.

Tre and Money D are at a club called, *La'Bay*, not far from the track. Money D tells Tre, "You're the luckiest man I know. How do you keep that many broads in check? I have problems keeping my one broad in check." Tre replies, "Most times they too busy trying to outdo each other, that's enough to keep them busy, I only have to gorilla pimp periodically." They both laugh. Tre says, "But on a serious note, the money on the track is way too slow, I've been watching the female named Beautiful, she is friends with my home girl Jackie. They should be sliding through here any minute, my girl Jackie said they were coming here tonight." Money D replies, "Ain't she with Dominic?" Tre says, "For now. She gets real money, she goes in them banks, and if she chooses, the rest is history." Money D replies, "I heard that, so how your other broads going to act, knowing she won't be working the track with them?" Tre tells Money D, "I'm a real pimp, which means there's only one way to act around me and that's in pocket, I don't tolerate nothing else. And whoever has a problem with my pimping, can keep it moving." They slap hands and laugh. Tre says, "I found out Beautiful been eye bawling me too." Money D replies, "It's your year, man." Tre says, "It looks that way." Jackie and Beautiful walk into *La'Bay*, looking good. Jackie has on a black one-piece romper pant outfit, with a black waist length leather coat, black and tan pointed toe shoes, with a black purse, and all gold jewelry. Beautiful is wearing a black satin coat dress with gold square shaped buttons on the cuffs of the sleeves of the dress, black heels with the toes out, and a black clutch purse, with all gold jewelry. They walk over to Tre's table. Jackie says, "How you gentlemen doing?" Tre replies, "Hey Jackie, why don't you and your friend have a seat." Jackie looks at Beautiful and says, "Are you cool with that?" Beautiful replies, "That's fine," and both ladies sit down. Jackie says, "Tre, this my girl Beautiful," then she asks Money D, "What's your name?" He replies, "Money D." Jackie responds, "Okay, I'm Jackie, so now that we've all been introduced, can we get a drink?" Beautiful says, "That's real talk." Money D asks them, "What are y'all drink-ing?" Jackie responds, "A Cadillac Margarita," and Beautiful says, "a Beautiful." Money D goes to the bar. Tre looks into Beautiful eyes and asks her, "Who you with?" She responds, "I was with Dominic, but now I'm single." Tre rubs his chin and says, "I like that." Jackie and Beautiful look at each other and smile. Beautiful replies, "Why you like the fact that I'm single?" Tre tells Beautiful, "I like what I see and the word on the street is that you a go-getter. I love those that have a desire like I do, to be a high achiever, and not scared to go after what they want." Beautiful replies, "Well, I heard about you too." Tre responds, "Well, that's good. I've been around

Richmond and the Bay Area most of my life. I would think you definitely would have heard something about me. Something good from my fans, and love ones, and something bad from my haters." Money D walks back up to the table, followed by a waitress carrying their drinks. The remainder of the night Beautiful and Tre are talking, drinking and laughing, as Jackie and Money D get a kick out of watching an O.G couple dance all night.

--$--

Precious is in the room getting dressed when her phone rings. She answers and says, "Hey cuz, I'm sorry I didn't call you back the other day." (pause) I just need to talk to you some time. Candy is cool, but there is only so much I can talk to her about when it comes to Tre." (pause) "I've been working these streets since I was 16 years old, and since Jazzy has been here, it's clearer to me that all pimps want from us is our money. How am I ever going to feel special when I'm in a relationship with him and two other women." (pause)

Precious is getting irritated, "I know I can leave, but I need to stack some money, and I need his protection on the streets. So, I'm going to start wiring you some money every few days to put up for me." (pause) "I know, reality hurts, and it's time for me to look out for my future." Precious hears Tre and Candy walk in the house and whispers, "Cuz, I have to go, I'll call you soon."

Tre has his finger in Candy's face and is yelling. Precious walks into the living room. Jazzy wakes up from being asleep on the couch. Tre says, "What's with you getting sloppy drunk on the track? "Candy says, "I only had a few drinks." Tre replies, "When you handling my business, there is no drinking. And that goes for all y'all. When you drunk, that's how the police catch you slipping. Let me find out y'all been drinking on the job, it's going to take a surgeon to get my shoe out of one of y'all. Y'all can play with my pimping and my money if you want to." Tre puts his finger closer in Candy's face, she is scared and flinches. Tre yells, "Go take a shower, get dressed and get to the track immediately, and go get my money I bailed you out with." As Candy rushes towards the room, Tre looks at Precious and Jazzy and says, "Let me even think one of y'all been drinking, you gonna work that track seven days straight with no rest. Y'all won't see the walls of this joint. Matter of fact, all y'all get dressed and get to work."

--$--

Beautiful and her mom are sitting on a park bench at Nicholas Park in Richmond. Beautiful's mom says, "So what have you been up to, baby?" Beautiful replies, "Mom, I been looking for jobs, but I'm just not feeling working for nobody, I want my own business." Beautiful's mom responds, "There's nothing wrong with you having your own business. But you need to go to college to learn how to run your own business, or at least go to a training school that specializes in teaching you how to run a business. Baby, for a while now I've been watching you, you been doing something you don't want me to know about. You have a new BMW, live in a plush condo, and, girl, I know that jewelry you wearing is very valuable. Beautiful, whatever you doing, you better stop." Beautiful replies, "Mom, I don't want to talk to you about my personal life." Beautiful mom says, "Okay, you are grown, but I'm going to leave you with this. Your pattern is dating men in the streets, and you always end up hustling for them. You need to realize that although you're not standing on the corner, pimping comes in all forms." Beautiful stands up, raises her voice and says, "I'm not a prostitute!" Her mom stands up and says, "Watch your tone!" Beautiful sits back down. Her mom says, "You can glamorize whatever you do, to try to make yourself feel better than someone that is out on the corner, but the reality is you aren't no better than them. Everything comes to an end. People been in the game and hustling since the game began, but the smart ones get out the streets and find what their passion is, and move on to do something productive with their life. Everybody at some point get tired of looking over their shoulder for the police, or for those that want to come to take what they think you got. But I'm not going to keep talking. You grown and I want you to be grown, when and if it all hits the fan. Don't come crying like a little girl, stand tall like a woman and take responsibility for your actions, then you will be grown, and we can really talk, cause you gonna want to really talk then." Beautiful replies, "Mama, I hear you, but I'm not stupid!" Beautiful's mom gets emotional and says, "I love you and I keep you in my prayers." Beautiful stands up, hugs her mom and says, "I love you too!" Beautiful's mom gently touches the side of her daughter's face and tells her, "Baby, think about what I said." Her mom grabs her purse and heads toward her car, then Beautiful leaves.

Beautiful immediately goes to Jackie's house after meeting with her mom. She and Jackie are sitting at the kitchen table. Beautiful says, "Girl, I just met with my mom and she was straight tripping." Jackie replies, "What happened?" Beautiful responds, "She was trying to compare what I do to being a prostitute! First of all, she doesn't know what I'm doing." Jackie tells her, "You my girl and I love you, but your mom is just keeping it real. I've seen you hustle, and buy dudes' cars, clothes, and jewelry, but they hardly do anything for you. I mean, they take you out to dinner, but you can do that for yourself." Beautiful says, "Square dudes are boring to me." Jackie replies, "Girl, when you get older, all the good men are going to be taken. Them square dudes are going to have their own businesses, or careers with 401K's, health benefits, and when they retire, they will have a retirement coming in every month. So, them squares are going to be looking really good in the end."

Beautiful tells her, "I think Tre has potential, he just needs me by his side." Jackie replies, "So you think he gonna give up pimping." Beautiful replies, "Eventually he will." Jackie responds, "So, you don't mind sleeping with him, although you know he sleeping with his employees? And I've heard some of them will sleep with a trick without a condom if the money is right, which puts them at risk for AIDS." Beautiful says, "I'm sure he wears condoms with them." Jackie replies, "Maybe in the beginning, how many pimps we know that have kids by their workers. Don't get me wrong, Tre my boy, but you my girl too." Beautiful responds, "I think he shobber than that." Jackie says, "For your sake, I hope he is too. But, if he isn't, you need to wear one." Beautiful smiles, shakes her head and replies, "Well, I'm about to go get dressed, we hooking up later." Jackie says, "Alright, girl, be safe."

--$--

Tre and his uncle, Uncle Cool, are sitting at *The Spot* on the track, having a drink. Uncle Cool says, "So, nephew, I really hope you have an exit plan for this pimp game." Tre replies, "Uncle Cool, my money ain't long enough for me to even think about exiting the game." Uncle Cool tells Tre, "I had the same frame of mind, and look where it got me." Tre says, "You doing alright, Unc." Uncle Cool replies, "Don't let appearances fool you. Just because I dress a certain way, have some nice pieces of jewelry, and flip a new ride every couple of years, don't mean I'm financially in a good place, that's the reason I wanted to sit down and give you some serious insight on this game. The bottom line is, you young now, but keep living. So, stack your money, I know a few cats that end up with kids by chicks they used to talk disrespectful to, beat them and spit on them. They would even make them sleep with their other broads, and let their partners sleep with them. I know these cats would never have imagined they would end up an old pimp, settling down with their employees. Periodically, when I run into some of them, they go to introduce me to their females and quickly remember, not only do I know her, I may have been one of her pimps, or on one of my wilder nights, they broad may have slept with my broad. And I can see the look on their faces, rather the disappointment in themselves, without them saying a word, because they know how bad we used to talk about them females. But they done slipped up and turned their work into a housewife." Tre responds, "I hear you, Unc, I'm game tight. I ain't going out like that." Uncle cool tells Tre, "I'm 100 percent certain they didn't think so either. But you have to be on your toes 24/7, because 23 hours ain't enough." They both slap hands. Uncle cool says, "Pimping comes in all forms, get your money. But have an exit plan, so when you close the door to the game, the other door is already open. Find something you're passionate about. There are plenty of brothers that get dependent on them females, they know the broad really don't need them, they need her. Don't let this game trick you too. Nephew, I don't have no retirement plan or no good solid woman, I thought they were too square for me. I didn't look out for my future. Don't play yourself like that, I know GOD gave you life for a bigger purpose than this. You, my nephew, I love you, work on that exit plan." They both stand up and embrace.

--$--

Tre and Beautiful are at the club *La'Bay* where they had their initial introduction, not far from the track. Beautiful takes a sip of her drink. Tre looks into her eyes and says, "So let me get right to the point, we been kicking it a lot and both seem to be feeling each other, so are you ready to be with Tre, baby." Beautiful is caught off guard and slightly blushes and replies, "Yea, I can handle it." Tre smiles and responds, "So you can handle me, huh!" Beautiful tells Tre, "I know how to take care of my man." So Tre asks, "So the condo you at, is that your spot or did Dominic rent that spot for you?" She replies, "That's my spot! I had that spot since I was 17 years old, and it was fully furnished, I've been hustling since I was 15 years old. I was living with my mom, and she didn't know I had my own place. On the weekends she thought I was staying at friend's houses, but I'd be at my apartment." Tre says, "So let's get us a good run in this game, so we can retire young." She replies, "I'm with that." Tre responds, "Good! We going to have to get them locks changed to your spot tomorrow." Beautiful says, "Alright." Money D walks into the club. Tre says, "Look, I have some business up, that's why I had you to follow me here, I want you to make it an early night, so you can be on your business in the morning. I might come through later, but I'll call you either way." She replies, "That's cool." Tre stands up and says, "Come, give me some love." Beautiful gets up and they hug, she grabs her purse and leaves. Tre and Money D slap hands. Money D says, "What's up, man?" Tre replies, "I done struck gold!" They both laugh. Money D asks, "So she chose?" Tre pops his shirt collars and replies, "Why not?" Money D says, "I know you hooking up with baby tonight?" Tre responds, "Nah, I'm gonna wait until them locks at her spot get changed tomorrow, and she going to get some money." They both laugh. Tre says, "Let's roll through the track and check on them broads, and make sure they getting that money." Money D replies, "For real, I need a new employee, at the rate my broad getting money I'm gonna be hiding my car from the repo man." They laugh and get up to leave. Tre tells Money D, "You need to be on the track recruiting 24/7."

Money D is standing outside the bar, *The Spot*, talking to his broad on the phone. "You don't have no money! Where you at? (pause) You got five minutes to get where I told you to be, and since you want to be out of pocket, you about to pull an all-nighter, so get comfortable! Get comfortable!" Money D hangs up the phone and walks to the bar.

Tre and Candy are sitting at a table at *The Spot*. Tre tells Candy, "You playing with my money and my pimping! I don't have time to be babysitting you on this track. What's on your mind that's interfering with my money? Even Jazzy is outshining you." Candy replies, "You never spend no time with me. It's like, I don't have no purpose in life." Candy gets emotional and is about to cry.

Tre says, "Check this out, I ain't changed and my rules haven't changed. I'm a pimp, not your boyfriend, I'm a businessman. This has always been business and I've expressed that from the start. Yea, I'm your man and every dude out here knows not to step to you. Have you had any problems?" Candy replies, "No." Tre asks, "Did I explain myself clearly when I told you what I stand for, and what my expectations were when you chose me?" Candy replies, "Yes." Tre asks her, "Are you homeless?" She says, "No." Tre replies, "Do you have a car?" Candy responds, "Yes." Tre says, "Do you have money?" Tre then holds his hand up and tells her, "But before you answer that, most pimps take all your money." Candy responds, "I know you good to me. But we don't spend no time together, I mean at least once a week, every other week, can we just be together? I been with you longer than Precious and Jazzy." Tre responds, "First of all, as with any employer and employee situation, the employee with the most seniority, especially in the private sector, does not automatically get a bonus every month. That employee has to work hard every month to get that bonus. So, upon me saying that, I will incorporate the employee of the month reward system." Candy starts smiling, and Tre continues to speak, "So the person that makes the most money will get something special from me, and that may be a little quality time. And since you have been with me the longest, you should be out here setting a better example, and being out here drinking every night ain't a positive example for nobody. And since you haven't been on my business correctly, from now on, when you and Jazzy get some money, give it to Precious." Candy stops smiling.

Tre continues to talk, "She seems to be more professional than you. And a word of advice, stop letting emotional issues get in the way of business." Tre looks at his watch and tells her, "Your break is up, get back to work."

--$--

Three months later, it's a big night, it's the Player's Ball. Pimps, and players from all over the Bay Area, are at the venue *Elegance* in Berkeley, California, it's at full capacity. The males and females are dressed to impress, wearing the finest of clothing, diamonds and gold jewelry, as well as fur hats and coats. The room is full of large circular tables, and two long tables at the front of the room with a podium in the middle where Silky an O.G pimp, who is the speaker for the players' ball, will announce the winners of this year's annual extraordinaire players ball. The music is playing and everyone is vibing to the music and talking at their tables.

Silky walks up to the podium in a black pinstripe suit with white stripes, a black brim with a thin white band around the hat, diamond cuff links with gold trimming, and black and white alligator shoes. Silky has on a gold chain with a diamond medallion, a diamond watch and a diamond and gold pinky ring. Silky says, "Gentlemen, all nominees, come have a seat at the two tables on either side of the podium." As the pimps take their seats, their females stand behind them. After the last person takes his seat, Silky tells everyone, "It's good to see all my fellow pimps and playas. Welcome to our 6th Annual Bay Area Playas Extraordinaire Ball." Silky hands his female his decorative cup and she hands him a trophy. Silky says, "So without further delay, our third prize winner is my partna, that's still holding it down. The Ultimate Mac, Mac Jay!" Mac Jay stands up and walks up to the podium and his two females follow him up. Mac Jay has a long perm and is wearing a turquoise suit with matching alligator shoes, and all gold jewelry. Silky and him embrace, and Silky hands him the trophy. Mac Jay says, "I'm going to address you, young playas, if this game is what you want, stay down 24/7, stay down." The crowd is clapping and Mac Jay goes back to his seat and his females follow him. Silky's female hands him another trophy as he steps back to the microphone. Silky says, "Our second prize winner is the one and only Gorilla G!" Gorilla G walks to the podium, wearing a black and gold suit, all gold jewelry, and gold alligator shoes, and his perm has curls that are hanging. His two females get up and follow him, and one of the females is walking on a cane due to her leg being messed up. Silky hands him the trophy. Gorilla G says, "Y'all know how I do it," and looks at his female with the broken leg, and says, "I'm a gorilla about mine! Till next year keep it pimping!" He then goes back to his spot at the table and his females follow. Silky's female hands him the last trophy as he goes back to the podium. Silky tells everyone, "My pimp partna and brother in this game is about to introduce the Bay Area Playa of the year, come up here, Cool." Uncle Cool walks up to the microphone, wearing a platinum suit with all custom diamond jewelry and a platinum brim and platinum alligator shoes, and a black floor length mink coat. They embrace and Silky hands him the trophy. Uncle Cool tells the crowd, "It's a special honor to introduce this boss playa, I was a big influence on this man getting in the game. Now for the moment we all been waiting for, the grand prize winner and playa of all playas of the 6th Annual Bay Area Playas Extraordinaire Ball is my nephew Tre!" The music starts playing, Tre walks up to the microphone wearing an all-leather white tailor-made suit, the jacket comes to his knees, he has on a diamond necklace with a diamond medallion, a diamond bracelet and a diamond ring, with diamond cuff links, and white leather alligator shoes, with a white mink hat. His three females follow him to the podium. Uncle Cool hands him the trophy and the two of them embrace. Tre's females are throwing money in the air and it's landing all over Tre and Uncle Cool. Cool steps to the side, and the music stops. Tre says, "Basically, my pimping speaks for itself. Playas, remember not to give the game a black eye, and it won't give you one back. Whether I would have received this trophy or not, I'm gonna continue to keep it real, and keep it solid! That speaks volumes about the playa that I am!" The music starts playing again and all the winners start embracing one another, and their females start dancing. The crowd is clapping and Tre's females walk to the center of the room and start dancing, while Tre and various pimps and playas in the room are embracing. Money D walks up and embraces Tre, and the two of them are side by side while all the playas in the room continue to embrace him and Tre, because everybody knows Money D is Tre's right hand. Many of the females at the Playas Ball are on the floor dancing with Tre's females, and the professional dancers are dancing on the stripper poles. This is definitely a gangsta party and everyone is drinking and partying! The ladies get a day off and the players get recognition, and some will get chosen! Yes, it's a good night for all boss players!

--$--

The next day, Precious is sitting on the couch looking out the window, and Candy walks into the room in sweats, a t-shirt and slippers holding her head. Candy asks, "Where is Jazzy?" Precious replies, "I guess she stayed with Tre, she stayed in the car when he dropped us off." Candy responded, "I don't even remember her staying in the car." Precious sarcastically replies, "I wonder why!" Candy says, "I was cele-brating with my man, he won Playa of the Year!" Precious replies, "You celebrate something every night." Candy says, "Whatever, I get money though!" Precious tells her, "Yeah, you make a few dollars. You good for the first three hours on the track. Huh, you ain't noticed you used to make three times the amount of money you pulling in now. Actually, do you know how much money you hand me every night since Tre been having you and Jazzy give me y'all money?" Candy looks puzzled and replies, "Yea, I know how much money I make." Precious asks, "How much?" Candy says, "I'm not going to justify that question with an answer." Precious laughs and replies, "Yea, right!" Candy looks at Precious crazy, then Candy's phone rings, she answers and says, "Hello." (pause) Candy responds, "Yea, this her." (pause) Candy looks puzzled and replies, "I'm on my way." Candy hangs up the phone and rushes to the bedroom. Precious yells, "Candy!" Candy quickly rushes from the room looking stressed, carrying her purse and coat, then tells Precious, "I have to go take care of some business." With a puzzled look, Precious replies, "Okay."

Precious pulls out her phone and calls her cousin, and whispers, "Hey cuz, you get the money I sent you?" (pause) Precious replies, "That's cool," then Jazzy enters the house. Precious says, "I'll talk to you later," and gets off the phone. Jazzy walks up to Precious and says, "Now, I know why y'all been with Tre so long." Precious stands up and points her finger in Jazzy's face and yells, "Whatever y'all did, is y'all business! "Jazzy sarcastically replies, with a smile on her face, "You right, you right."

--$--

It's evening, the day after the player's ball, Tre and Beautiful are at the club, *La'Bay*. Beautiful says, "I missed you staying at the house last night." Tre replies, "It was a long night, I won Playa of the Year." Beautiful smiles and says, "I heard, everybody knows, congratulations!" Tre says, "Thank you, baby." Beautiful pulls out an envelope and hands it to Tre. She is excited and tells him, "I tore em up today!" They both laugh and Tre says, "Good job, you definitely doing your part." Beautiful replies, "I know you celebrated last night, but I want to celebrate with my man too." Tre responds, "Yea, we can do that, have you had dinner?" Beautiful replies, "No." Tre says, "We gonna go to the city, and have dinner and drinks, let's roll." She leans over, gives Tre a kiss and replies, "Okay, I love San Francisco." Tre takes out some money, lays it on the table and they leave.

--$--

Two weeks later, Candy is in the house, lying on the couch with her face displaying a look of stress, she is having a cocktail and holding back tears. Jazzy walks into the house, looks at her and asks, "Why are you crying." Candy replies, "I'm okay, you better go get dressed, so we can get to the track." Jazzy tells Candy, "We got time, you look like you haven't slept in a week." Candy ignores her question but asks, "Have you seen Precious?" Jazzy replies, "Not since this morning." Candy picks up her phone and calls Precious. Candy looks shocked and says, "Precious phone is disconnected!" Candy walks to the bedroom. Jazzy quickly grabs her cell phone, calls Tre and says, "Tre, we getting ready for work, and Precious isn't here, and her phone is disconnected. "Candy rushes back to the living room and yells, "All Precious stuff is gone!" Jazzy, looking surprised, tells Tre, "Candy said all Precious stuff is gone!" (pause) Jazzy looks irritated and says, "Okay," and hangs up the phone, then says, "He told us to get dressed and go to work." Candy is extremely frustrated, Jazzy and her go to their rooms and get dressed.

The next evening, Tre and money D are sitting at a table at the bar, *The Spot*. Money D asks, "Ain't no word ringing on the streets about Precious?" Tre replies, "I'm not going to let no broad stop me, I'm a pimp. If she gone, there's somebody out there dying to be with a major playa like me." (pause) "The three years I had her, I ain't never eased up off my pimping. That's why I don't sympathize with none of them broads. When I get 'em, I work 'em hard, cause it ain't no telling when they gone bounce. Hey man, it is what it is." Money D says, "I couldn't have said it better." Tre responds, "Let's hit this track, I need another broad to make up for this loss." Money D replies, "I need some more work too!"

--$--

A month later, Jazzy is lying on the couch and Candy walks in and says, "You show been sleeping a lot lately." (silence) Jazzy sits up and Candy continues, "How long has it been since the Playas Ball?" Jazzy replies, "About a month and a half." Candy responds, "You better go get a pregnancy test." Jazzy is scared and responds, "I bought one already." Candy replies, "And?" Jazzy says, "I'm pregnant." Candy asks, "Have you told Tre?" Jazzy replies, "No, I'm scared. I want my baby and I think he gonna tell me to get an abortion." Candy raises her voice and says, "You better tell him, if you don't, I am! I'm not going to have him going bad on me." Jazzy replies, "I'm going to tell him! Please don't say nothing, let me tell him." Candy tells her, "Alright, you better tell him by tomorrow." Jazzy responds, "Okay."

--$--

The next night, Tre is at the bar, *The Spot,* having a drink, Jazzy walks in and sits across from Tre. He asks her, "So what's so important?" (pause) Jazzy's leg is shaking under the table, she is shifting in her chair, and she keeps rubbing her forehead. Speaking very low, she says, "I'm pregnant." Tre doesn't hear her and responds, "What? Speak up!" Jazzy replies, "I'm pregnant." Tre says, "What? The condom busted when you were working?" Jazzy replies, "No, Tre, I got pregnant the night of the Playas Ball, we didn't use a condom." (pause) Tre tells her, "I'm a pimp, I'm not having no kids right now." Jazzy's eyes begin to water and she is holding back tears. Tre raises his voice and says, "Get back to work, we ain't gonna speak on this issue right now." While Jazzy is leaving, Money D walks up and sits down. Tre is shaking his head. Money D says, "What's up?" Tre replies, "Jazzy just left here hollering she pregnant." Money D puts his hand up to his mouth and replies, "Ooh!" Tre responds, "That broad ain't having no baby by me, she getting an abortion." Money D says, "I know that's right." Jazzy runs into the bar upset and tells Tre, "Somebody just called me and said that Candy just passed out and they called 911!" Tre is highly irritated and replies, "She probably drunk!" Tre tells Jazzy to go back to work. Tre shakes his head, stands up and says, "Man, I'm about to go see what's going on with Candy." Money D says, "I'll roll with you," and they leave.

Two days later, Beautiful and Jackie are sitting at the club, *La'Bay*. Jackie asks her, "How are things with you and Tre?" Dominic walks into the club and walks toward them. Beautiful replies, "Everything is going cool." Dominic interrupts and says, "So how are you ladies doing?" They are shocked to see him. Jackie replies, "Hey, Dominic." Beautiful responds, "When did you get out?" Dominic says, "A couple of nights ago," then he slightly raises his voice and says, "Come take a ride with me. I need to talk to you." Beautiful replies, "We can talk right here," then looks at Jackie and tells her, "I'm going to talk to him for a minute." Jackie looks at Dominic crazy, grabs her drink and her purse, and walks toward the bar. Dominic points at Jackie and asks Beautiful, "Why she has an attitude with me?" She replies, "The way you just raised your voice, she probably thinks you gonna be tripping, since I broke up with you when you were in jail." He responds, "I ain't gonna lie, I was tripping, but it was more about you getting with somebody else. Tre in the game too, so why you couldn't just wait for me?" She replies, "Yea, you in the game, but all your money and the money I gave you was going up your nose, and to partying all the time." Dominic sniffs through his nose and says, "Yea, I have issues and I know what they are, but you cool with Tre about to have a baby with his worker Jazzy?!" She replies, "Yea, right!" Dominic says, "You don't have to believe me, she out on the track running her mouth about being pregnant by him." Beautiful doesn't say a word, but is shocked and trying not to show Dominic she is upset. Beautiful gets up to leave and Jackie follows, and Dominic sits there with a grin on his face.

A month and a half after Precious left Tre, Precious and her cousin Nena are at Precious' hair salon in Atlanta, Georgia. Nena is looking around in amazement. Nena says, "Cousin, you did it, you have your own hair salon. You never let go of your dream, and you really left Tre!" Precious replies, "In the beginning, I really believed he loved me, I thought I was special, but over the years reality set in, and what he loved was the fact that I was making money for him. "

Nena tells her, "If I had a few of y'all bringing me that money, I would have told y'all, I love y'all too. And, oh yea, y'all was special alright, giving him all y'all money." They both laugh, and Precious says, "But seriously, I had to sneak to go to hair school." Nena replies, "Yea, that's crazy." Precious responds, "I know there's going to be a lot of young girls coming to get their hair done, and if I can save one of them from going through some of what I went through, then I've done my job. I have a few things to do before I have my grand opening, but I'll be open in about a month." Nena says, "But look at you now! Look at GOD!" Precious replies, "Yes, let's go get some food before you have me in here crying. And when are you going to finish hair school?" Nena responds, "I am, don't start, Precious!" Precious smiles and shakes her head.

Tre and Uncle Cool are at the bar, *The Spot*. Tre is stressed and says, "Financially I'm gonna be hurting in a few months, I mean, I got some money put up, but with Candy being in the hospital, and then Beautiful bounced once she found out about Jazzy being pregnant. I've been trying to stack every dime Jazzy been bringing me." Uncle Cool replies, "Nephew, that's why I've stayed in your ear about getting out the game. When I was young, my dad used to tell me, there ain't no better feeling than making your own money. I didn't listen, and honestly, he had the real game, so it's time for you to take it and run with it." Jackie walks in and goes over to Tre and says, "Excuse me, I thought you might want to know that Beautiful is in jail." Tre asks, "For what?" Jackie says, "For going up in them banks." Tre replies, "Wow!" Jackie says, "Alright Tre, I'll see you around." He replies, "For sho," and she walks away. His uncle tells him, "I know she not with you no more, but I told you, nephew, it doesn't pay to depend on nobody but yourself." Tre shakes his head and takes a sip of his drink.

--$--

Tre comes into the house, sees Jazzy sleeping on the couch and yells, "Get up and get ready for work! I don't care about you being pregnant. You ain't having it! I made an appointment for you to get an abortion on Friday, and stop running your mouth on the track." Tre is angry and walks closer to Jazzy. Tre continues to speak, "You out there telling everybody you pregnant."

Tre's phone rings, he answers and says, "Hello." (pause) "Candy, when are you getting out the hospital?" (pause) "I need my money." (pause) "Tell me now?" Tre sits down next to Jazzy, with a surprise look on his face, and says, "You got AIDS!" (pause) Jazzy folds her arms together and starts rocking back and forth. Tre replies, "Yea, I'm here." (pause) Then he says, "I'll be up there." Tre hangs up the phone and walks out the door.

--$--

A month later, Tre and Money D are sitting at the bar, *The Spot*. Money D says, "Man, you really about to leave town?" Tre replies, "Yea, man, Candy is making progress, but I'm not sitting around waiting for nobody but myself. And as for Jazzy, she on her own, if she has the baby and it's mine, I'll take care of it, but when it comes to me and her, she knew what it was when she got with me." Money D says, "For real." Tre tells Money D, "Man, I need a new atmosphere, by myself, so I can focus. So I can seriously work on my master plan, which will ultimately be my exit plan." Tre stands up, Money D stands up and they embrace. Money D tells Tre, "Man, call me if you have any problems that need to be handled." Tre replies, "You know, I'm gonna call my right hand! Money D sits back down. Tre leaves, gets in his car, which is right in front of *The Spot*, starts his car, turns up the music and drives away.

The End

About the Author

Aleasher Hightower grew up in Richmond, California. At an early age, she loved telling stories to the neighborhood children.

As an adult, she continued to pursue her passion for writing. She began writing stage plays and producing her plays.

The Vallejo Times Herald wrote an article on her May 1, 2009, when she produced her first play titled, "The Power of Influence."

She then wrote her next stage play titled, "Oh! How Things Change!" which was performed at several locations, one being the Empress Theatre in Vallejo, CA. on July 22, 2017. She later turned this play into a screenplay, and now a book.

Aleasher considers herself an observer of life, which allows her to create narratives that she believes will enlighten others.

THOUGHTS, RANTS, POEMS, SOME SATIRE AND CRAZY WORDS FROM MY HEAD #2

After years in the automotive business, in and around the United States, I moved to the desert of Southern Utah.

It was in early 2018 where the red rocks of the area inspired some hidden creativity.

I started to write poetry. I had a goal to write one poem every day, with a serious wonder if it could be done, at least by me.

Well, almost three years later, and close to 800 poems, rants, thoughts, and crazy words have been written.

Who would have thought that an old Harley riding, mountain biking, serious powder, and mogel skier had any creative juices inside his head?

I hope you enjoy my thoughts and get some mind fulfillment reading my words linked together to form these books.

Thank You;